RUBBER EGG

Kitchen Experiment

By Meg Gaertner

Published by The Child's World®
1980 Lookout Drive • Mankato, MN 56003-1705
800-599-READ • www.childsworld.com

Photographs ©: Rick Orndorf, cover, 1, 14, 16, 17, 18, 19,
20, 21; Martine Doucet/iStockphoto, 5; iStockphoto, 6, 7, 12;
Rob Mattingley/iStockphoto, 9; Shutterstock Images, 11

ISBN 9781503825376
LCCN 2017959698

Printed in the United States of America
PA02378

Table of Contents

CHAPTER 1

Inside an Egg

Some animals grow inside eggs before they are born. Chickens, ducks, lizards, and fish all grow inside eggs. Some animals lay eggs that do not have a baby animal growing inside. Chickens will lay eggs that do not have chicks inside. We can eat those eggs.

There are four main parts of an egg. The yellow part of the egg is called the yolk. Before an egg hatches, the yolk supplies food for the animal. The yolk helps it grow.

Chickens often lay their eggs in a coop. We can gather the eggs we want to eat.

The other part inside the egg is the egg white. The egg white protects the yolk. We can eat both the yolk and the egg white. But we have to break the eggshell and membrane first.

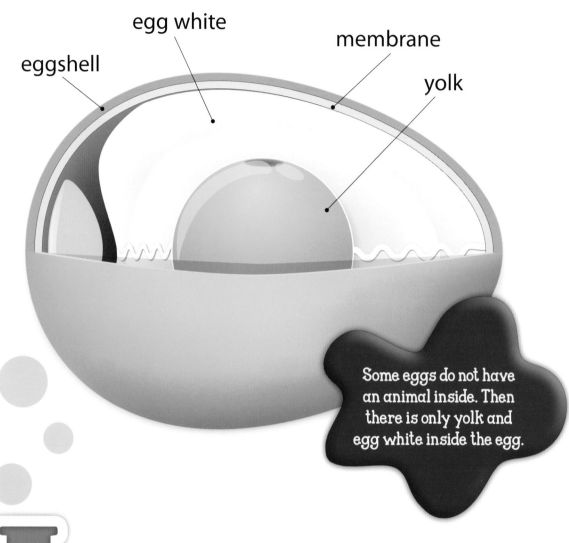

eggshell

egg white

membrane

yolk

Some eggs do not have an animal inside. Then there is only yolk and egg white inside the egg.

TIP

In a raw egg, the egg white is clear. It only becomes white when you cook it!

The membrane of an egg is like its skin. It keeps the egg white and yolk inside. The eggshell is hard. It keeps the egg safe.

Calcium helps our bones grow. Doctors can look at our bones using an x-ray machine.

Our bones are like eggshells. Bones are made of calcium. Calcium makes our bones hard and strong.

An eggshell is made of calcium carbonate. Calcium carbonate is found in rocks. It is also in some animal shells. Acids can break down calcium carbonate. This means the calcium carbonate is no longer there.

CHAPTER 2

An Egg with No Shell

Have you seen a raw egg break? The yolk and egg white spill out of the shell and membrane. It is very messy. How about a boiled egg? You can break the shell and eat the egg inside.

You can also get rid of the eggshell without breaking the membrane. The egg will be hard. But it will also still be raw. You can make a hard, raw egg by putting it in vinegar. Vinegar is made of water and acetic acid.

We break raw eggs when we cook with them.

That acid will get rid of the calcium carbonate of the eggshell.

The egg yolk and egg white do not break through. Why not? The membrane still covers the egg. It will become hard. It will feel like rubber. This is because vinegar enters the egg.

The membrane lets water flow through it. Why does water move through membranes? Water moves from places of high concentration to places of low concentration. It moves to make the same concentration of water on both sides of the membrane.

An egg soaked in vinegar will feel like it is made of rubber. Some balls are made of rubber.

11

Vinegar is used in cooking. Pickles are made with cucumbers and vinegar.

Concentration is how much of something there is. Vinegar has a high concentration of water. It is mostly water. An egg has a low concentration of water. It has less water in it. Water from the vinegar will move into the egg.

The egg will get bigger because of the added water. The membrane will still protect the egg. You can gently bounce a rubber egg from a few inches above a surface without the egg breaking.

TIP
Corn syrup has an even lower concentration of water than an egg. If you put an egg in corn syrup, it will get smaller.

CHAPTER 3

THE EXPERIMENT
Let's Make a Rubber Egg!

MATERIALS LIST

1 egg
1 glass or jar
1 cup (237 mL) vinegar
a few drops of food coloring

TIME TO PREPARE: 5 minutes

5

TIME TO COMPLETE:
5 days

1. Hold the egg in your hand. How does the egg feel? Is it hard or soft?
2. Gently put the egg in the glass.

3. Add the vinegar to the glass. Vinegar should cover the whole egg.

4. Add a few drops of food coloring to the glass.

5. Put the egg in a safe space. Leave the egg in the glass for five days.

6. After five days, take the egg out of the vinegar. Be very gentle with the egg so it does not break. Carefully peel off any last pieces of the shell. Rinse off the egg with water.

7. Hold the egg a few inches above a table. Then let it go. Watch the egg bounce.

TIP
Be careful! The egg will still break if you bounce it too hard.

8. Gently press on the sides of the egg.
   Does it feel different than it did when
   you began?

9. Wash your hands with soap and water after
   touching the egg or the vinegar. Raw eggs
   can make you sick. Vinegar will sting if you
   rub your eyes.

Glossary

acetic acid (uh-SEE-tik ASS-id) Acetic acid is an acid. Acetic acid is mixed with water to make vinegar.

acids (ASS-ids) Acids give off a lot of hydrogen atoms. Acids can make an eggshell disappear.

calcium (KAL-see-uhm) Calcium is an element. Calcium is found in bones and shells.

calcium carbonate (KAL-see-uhm CAR-buhn-ate) Eggshells are made of calcium carbonate. Calcium carbonate protects the egg.

concentration (kon-suhn-TRAY-shuhn) Concentration is how much of something there is. Vinegar has a high concentration of water.

egg white (EG WITE) An egg white is the clear part inside an egg. An egg white is only white when cooked.

eggshell (EG-shel) An eggshell is the hard layer around an egg. An eggshell keeps the egg safe.

membrane (MEM-brayn) A membrane is a thin skin. A membrane covers the egg white and yolk of an egg.

yolk (YOKE) The yolk is the yellow part of an egg. The yolk is food for a growing animal.

To Learn More

In the Library

Akass, Susan. *My First Science Book*. New York, NY: CICO Books, 2015.

Markovics, Joyce. *Chicken*. New York, NY: Bearport, 2017.

Merritt, Robin. *The Life Cycle of a Chicken*. Mankato, MN: The Child's World, 2012.

On the Web

Visit our Web site for links about rubber eggs:
childsworld.com/links

Note to Parents, Teachers, and Librarians: We routinely verify our Web links to make sure they are safe and active sites. So encourage your readers to check them out.

Index

About the Author

Meg Gaertner is a children's book author and editor who lives in Minnesota. When not writing, she enjoys dancing and spending time outdoors.